Dear Parent:
Your child's love of reading starts here!

Every child learns to read in a different way and at his or her own speed. You can help your young reader improve and become more confident by encouraging his or her own interests and abilities. You can also guide your child's spiritual development by reading stories with biblical values and Bible stories, like I Can Read! books published by Zonderkidz. From books your child reads with you to the first books he or she reads alone, there are I Can Read! books for every stage of reading:

SHARED READING
Basic language, word repetition, and whimsical illustrations, ideal for sharing with your emergent reader.

BEGINNING READING
Short sentences, familiar words, and simple concepts for children eager to read on their own.

READING WITH HELP
Engaging stories, longer sentences, and language play for developing readers.

READING ALONE
Complex plots, challenging vocabulary, and high-interest topics for the independent reader.

ADVANCED READING
Short paragraphs, chapters, and exciting themes for the perfect bridge to chapter books.

I Can Read! books have introduced children to the joy of reading since 1957. Featuring award-winning authors and illustrators and a fabulous cast of beloved characters, I Can Read! books set the standard for beginning readers.

A lifetime of discovery begins with the magical words **"I Can Read!"**

Visit www.icanread.com for information on enriching your child's reading experience.
Visit www.zonderkidz.com for more Zonderkidz I Can Read! titles.

This is the day the LORD has made;
let us rejoice and be glad in it.

—Psalm 118:24

The children's group
of Zondervan

www.zonderkidz.com

Jake Goes Fishing
Copyright © 2007 by Crystal Bowman
Illustrations © 2007 by Karen Maizel
Originally published in *Jonathan James Says, "School's Out"* © 1997
ISBN-10: 0-310-71454-0
ISBN-13: 978-0-310-71454-5

Requests for information should be addressed to:
Grand Rapids, Michigan 49530

Library of Congress Cataloging-in-Publication Data

Bowman, Crystal.
   Jake goes fishing / story by Crystal Bowman ; pictures by Karen Maizel.
     p. cm. – (Jake Biblical values series) (I can read! level 2)
   Summary: Although he makes some mistakes at first, Jake spends
a wonderful day fishing with his father, then enjoying a very special
fish dinner.
   ISBN-13: 978-0-310-71454-5 (softcover)
   ISBN-10: 0-310-71454-0 (softcover)
   [1. Fishing–Fiction. 2. Fathers and sons–Fiction. 3. Christian life
–Fiction.]   I. Maizel, Karen, ill. II. Title.
PZ7.B68335Jah 2007
[E]–dc22
                         2006029330

Art Direction: Laura Maitner-Mason
Cover and Interior Design: Jody Langley

Printed in China

07 08 09 10 11 • 10 9 8 7 6 5 4 3 2 1

Jake Goes Fishing

story by Crystal Bowman

pictures by Karen Maizel

Jake woke up very early.

Father put the fishing poles

in the red truck.

They drove to Sunfish Lake.

"I hope we catch some big fish

for supper tonight," said Jake.

"That would be nice," Father said.

Father gave Jake a box.

"You carry the worms, Jake," he said.

"I'll carry the fishing poles."

Jake and Father walked
down a steep hill toward the lake.
Plop! Jake tripped and fell.

He dropped the worms.

"Oh, no!" cried Jake.

"The worms are crawling away!"

"Well," said Father.

"We can't have a fish supper

if we don't have worms."

"I'll pick them up," said Jake.

Father and Jake picked up the worms

and put them back in the box.

"Let's get in the boat," said Father.

Father rowed the fishing boat

to the middle of the lake.

"How do you know where to go?"

Jake asked Father.

"I know a secret spot," he said.

"And we are almost there."

"Yippee! It's time to fish!"
shouted Jake.

"Shhh," whispered Father.

"We can't have a fish supper
if we scare all the fish away."

"Sorry," said Jake.

Father gave Jake a fishing pole.

He put a worm on the hook.

"Put it in the water," said Father.

Jake tried to fish like Father,

but the hook caught on his pants.

"Help!" cried Jake.

"Let me help," said Father.

"We can't have a fish supper

if your worm isn't in the water."

Father took the hook

out of Jake's pants.

Jake and Father sat in the boat

and held their poles.

They waited and waited and waited.

"I've got a fish!" said Father.

"It's a big one!" said Jake.

"Pull it up! Pull it up!"

Father reeled in his fish and put it in the pail.

"That's one for supper!" he said.

Jake felt a tug on his pole.

"I've got one! I've got one!"

he yelled.

Jake reeled in his fish

and put it in the pail.

"That's two for supper!" he said.

They fished all morning long.

Father caught three fish.

Jake caught four fish.

"It was fun catching
all those fish," said Jake.

"We have lots of fish
for our fish supper," said Father.

Then Jake felt sad.

"I don't want to eat the fish,"

he told Father.

"I want to put them in the lake."

"Are you sure?" asked Father.

"We can't have a fish supper

without the fish."

"Yes, I'm sure," said Jake.

27

Father put the pail in the water.

Jake watched the fish swim away.

"I spoiled everything," he said.

"Now we won't have a fish supper."

"You didn't spoil anything, Jake,"

said Father.

"God gave us a beautiful day.

We had lots of fun together.

That's the most important thing."

Father stopped at the grocery store.

Jake found a box of crackers.

They were shaped like little fish.

"Look!" he said. "Fish for supper!"

"That would be nice," said Father.

At dinnertime,

Jake put the crackers in a bowl

and set them on the table.

Then he bowed his head to pray.

"Thank you, God, for this fun day

and for our fish supper."

"Amen," said Father. "Let's eat!"